Given to:

With Love By:

I'm going to be a Big Cousin!

Guess what I heard? I'll tell you, it's great!

A new cousin is coming,
it is time to celebrate!

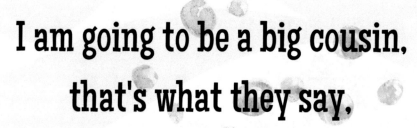

I am going to be a big cousin,
that's what they say,

And I can't hardly wait for this very special day!

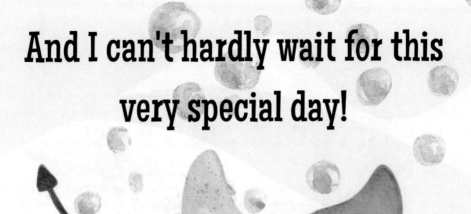

I'll teach my new cousin
games and how to explore.

I'll show them all sorts of fun things and so much more.

I'll read them stories,
we will sing songs aloud,

Being a big cousin
will make me feel proud!

I'll be there to help
keep them safe,
I'll hold their hand tight,

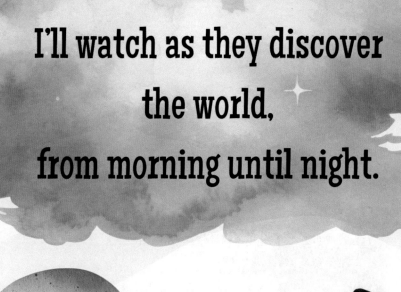

I'll watch as they discover
the world,
from morning until night.

I'll share my toys
and all I know,

Being a big cousin,
I'll do all I can to
help them learn and grow!

Little cousins are great,
I know this is true,

They bring joy and fun
in all that they do.

I'm so excited! A baby cousin,
so tiny and new,
I will wrap them in love,
it'll be a dream come true.

They will make life better, right from the start!

I can't wait to meet my
new cousin,
I'm sure they will have a
beautiful heart.

Hooray!
I'm going
to be a
Big
Cousin!

The End

Made in the USA
Monee, IL
26 December 2024

75382686R00017